RETURN TO THE LIBRARY OF DOOM

RATS ON THE PAGE

BY MICHAEL DAHL

ILLUSTRATED BY
BRADFORD KENDALL

Raintree

www.raintreepublishers.co.uk
Visit our website to find out
more information about
Raintree books.

To order:
☎ Phone 0845 6044371
🖷 Fax +44 (0) 1865 312263
🖳 Email myorders@raintreepublishers.co.uk

Customers from outside the UK please telephone +44 1865 312262

Raintree is an imprint of Capstone Global Library Limited, a company
incorporated in England and Wales having its registered office at 7 Pilgrim
Street, London, EC4V 6LB – Registered company number: 6695582

Text © Stone Arch Books 2011
First published in the United Kingdom in hardback and paperback by
Capstone Global Library Ltd in 2011
The moral rights of the proprietor have been asserted.

Art Director: Kay Fraser
Graphic Designer: Hilary Wacholz
Production Specialist: Michelle Biedscheid
Originated by Capstone Global Library Ltd
Printed in and bound in China by Leo Paper Products Ltd

ISBN 978 1 406 22507 5 (hardback)
15 14 13 12 11
10 9 8 7 6 5 4 3 2 1

ISBN 978 1 406 22514 3 (paperback)
15 14 13 12 11
10 9 8 7 6 5 4 3 2 1

British Library Cataloguing in Publication Data
A full catalogue record for this book is available from the British Library.

Contents

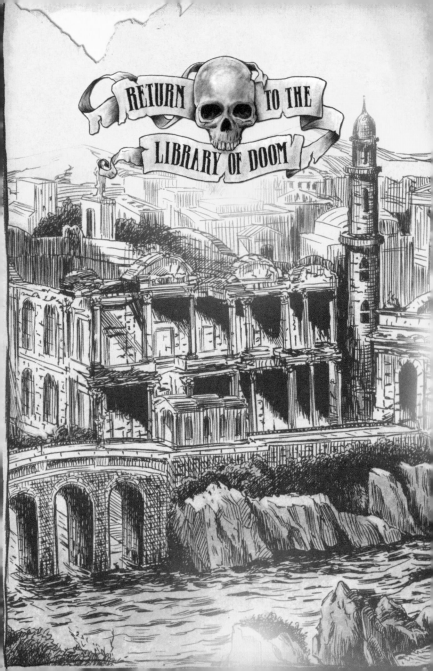

Behold the Library of Doom! The world's largest collection of deadly and dangerous books. Only the Librarian can prevent these books from falling into the hands of those who would use them for evil.

WHAT HAPPENS WHEN SOMETHING DECIDES THAT BOOKS ARE GOOD TO EAT?

Chapter 1

IN THE ALLEY

Two boys *rummage* through rubbish bins.

"Find anything good?" asks the SMALLER boy.

The older boy, named Alex, shakes his head.

"But look at this," he says.

Reaching deep inside the bin, Alex pulls out a **LARGE**, thick book.

He drops it on the floor of the alley.

"Don't do that!" says Mattie, the smaller boy. "It might be valuable. We could sell it for a lot of **MONEY**." £

£

£

£

£

£

The covers are made of smooth, dark leather. The edges of the pages SHINE like gold.

"Rats!" says Alex.

The smaller boy looks over his shoulder. His eyes search the DARK corners of the alley.

"I hate those FURRY things!" Mattie says.

Alex laughs. "Don't be **scared**," he says. "I meant the book."

He points to the old leather cover.

Mattie looks **CLOSER**.

"Who'd want to read a book about rats?" he says.

Then he sees something sticking out from the pages.

A **TAIL**.

Chapter 2

FURRY PAGES

Mattie **JUMPS** back from the book.

Alex laughs again. "It's only string,"
he says. He opens the book and pulls on
the tail. "It's a **fake** rat. See?"

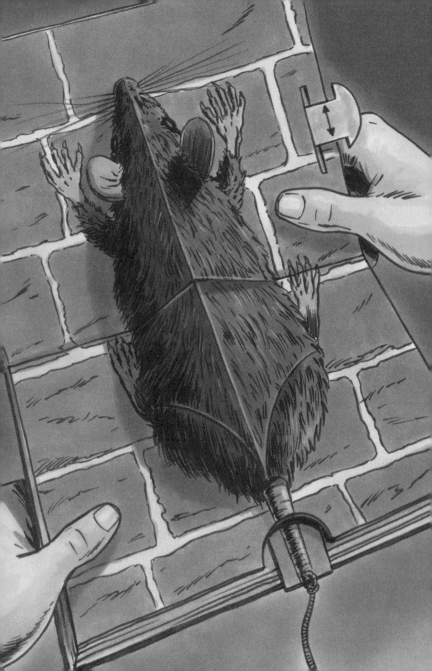

When Alex pulls the tail, a paper
rat moves its FEET.

"Cool!" says Mattie. "I bet we could
sell this and make a lot of money!"

Mattie REACHES down and
strokes the fake fur.

"It feels really soft," says Mattie.

"Let's get out of here," says Alex.

"I'm still hungry."

Alex starts walking down the alley.

Then he hears a loud **SQUEAK**
behind him.

"Al!" CRIES Mattie.

Mattie holds out his arm.

It is **covered** in rat-coloured fur.

Chapter 3

RAT BOY

Alex's eyes grow wide with **HORROR**.

Mattie hunches over on the floor of the alley. He feels **sick**.

Fur spreads across his back and legs.

His fingers sprout hard, yellow nails.

Mattie's face **GROWS** long and hairy.

Whiskers bloom on each side of his nose.

His **EYES** are dark and shiny.

"Mattie!" yells Alex.

Suddenly, the **RAT BOY** jumps away from the book.

He SCAMPERS down the alley on four furry legs.

"Come back!" yells the older boy.

He follows the rat boy through the

TWISTING alley.

As Alex runs, he sees other rats

running in the same **direction**.

The alley is soon **filled** with the furry creatures.

Alex can't tell his friend apart from the other **RODENTS**.

Finally, the all rats stop. They sniff the air.

Alex hears a WHISTLING sound.

The sound seems to come from a dark opening in the alley.

It is a manhole with its cover missing.

One by one, the rats throw themselves into the manhole.

Alex watches as their flicking tails disappear into the darkness. Soon, there is only **ONE** rat left.

The last RAT squeaks and squeaks.

It stares at Alex.

Its dark, shiny eyes blink with fear.

"Mattie?" asks Alex.

The rat DIVES into the opening.

Alex steps closer to the manhole.

He sees the metal rungs of a ladder.

Without a pause, the boy climbs
into the dark hole.

He must FIND his friend.

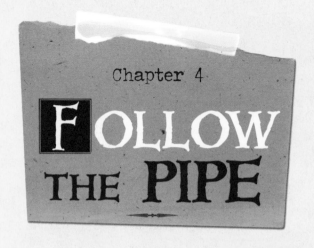

Chapter 4

FOLLOW THE PIPE

Alex follows the sound of tiny feet.

The **scratching** and scraping of the rats echo through the large sewer pipes.

Soon, Alex is swallowed up in **darkness**.

He stretches his arms out on either side to feel his way.

His **fingers** brush the cold, damp bricks of the tunnel walls.

His shoes squish through a trickle of dirty **water**.

Squeak! Squeak!

He hears the cries of the rats in the distance.

The whistling sound has grown louder.

A dim **LIGHT** glows up ahead.

Finally, Alex enters a gigantic room.

"Mattie," calls Alex, quietly.

"Mattie, where are you?"

There are more and more rats. They cover the floor like a moving, **living** <u>CARPET</u>.

The rats climb over stone benches. They wade through empty fountains. They **SCURRY** on to shelves and nibble on the books.

HA

HA

HA

Alex hears someone laughing.

HA

Carefully, the boy creeps past the feasting rats.

From behind a large bookcase, Alex sees a **MAN** standing in the centre of the huge room.

The man is old and thin. His eyes GLOW like red flames.

In one claw-like hand he holds a flute. In the other, he holds a lead.

At the end of the lead is a **GIANT**, angry rat.

The rat gives a fierce **shake** of his lead.

"Don't worry, my pet," says the man. "I know that your little friends will soon eat all the books in this chamber. But there are many more rooms in the Library of Doom. It will take years before my rats run out of food! And there is no one to stop them!"

Chapter 5

THE MAGIC FLUTE

The man holds the flute to his lips.

He plays a **WEIRD** tune. The rats seem to move to the music.

The man plays faster and faster, and the rats twitch their tails. They are **nibbling** faster and faster on the books.

How will I ever find Mattie? wonders Alex. *There must be* **HUNDREDS** *of rats in here.*

There are a thousand.

And **each** one is chewing on a priceless book.

Except for one rat. The giant rat on the man's leash struggles and **squirms.**

The man keeps playing his tune.

That rat doesn't look happy, thinks Alex. *I wonder what it does like to eat?*

The flute **STOPS** playing.

The man is looking into the air.

Alex turns to follow the man's gaze. He sees a **STRANGE** woman flying above them.

"Call **OFF** your beasts, Spellbinder," the woman demands. "And return these children to their original forms!"

The man's lips twist in an evil grin. "Try to stop me, Skywriter," sneers the man. "You can't fight against a **thousand!**"

Chapter 6

The Spellbinder quickly plays a few **NOTES** on his flute. The rats stop nibbling.

A thousand tails stop **TWITCHING**. A thousand pairs of dark eyes gaze at Skywriter.

Skywriter smiles and **leaps** into the air.

"You forget that I can fly," she says to the **evil** magician.

"Yes, I know you can," replies the man. "But I also know that he can't!"

He points a **BONY** finger at Alex.

The rats run towards the boy.

Alex **SCREAMS** and covers his face with his arms. Something touches his wrists. "Ah!" he yells.

"Don't be scared," says Skywriter.

Alex keeps screaming as the woman LIFTS him into the air.

The rats leap at his **wiggling** legs. Their claws try to grab his feet.

The woman looks down at the **frightened** boy.

"You've given me an idea," she says.

She rises higher and higher above the rat **SWARM**. Then she opens her mouth.

The rats don't move. They are silent.

Alex doesn't hear a thing.

The **WOMAN** seems to be screaming, but no sound comes from her throat.

Then the rats begin to scream. "EEEEEE!"

The scream of the rats GROWS louder and louder.

Alex wants to cover his ears, but
Skywriter is still holding his wrists.

Then the Spellbinder's flute **shatters**.

The Spellbinder drops the lead.

He flees into the shadows of the
furthest bookshelves.

As the broken flute falls to the floor,
the rats begin to shake.

The rats shiver and shudder. Their
tails begin to SHRINK.

Alex looks down and sees Mattie **WAVING** at him.

The rats have disappeared. The floor of the library chamber is now `covered` with hundreds and hundreds of children.

A **THOUSAND** of them.

Skywriter returns Alex gently to the floor.

Alex looks around quickly. "What happened to that GIANT rat?" he asks.

Skywriter points behind them.

Alex and Mattie turn and see another man. "This lead is a little too **tight**," he says.

"This is the Librarian," says the woman. "He is the guardian of the Library of Doom."

The two HEROES raise their arms and torches appear out of the air. "Follow us!" they shout to the children.

A thousand pairs of feet paddle through the pipes and return to their homes.

Soon, Alex and Mattie are back in the ALLEY.

"How did you make the rats scream?" Alex asks.

"I made a sound that only they could hear," explains Skywriter. "The sound I made was much worse than theirs. That is why they SCREAMED."

"And the vibrations **shattered** the evil flute," adds the Librarian.

"But you were so quiet," says Alex.

Skywriter smiles. "You're supposed to be <u>QUIET</u> in a library, remember?" she says.

The two heroes dissolve into the **DARKNESS**.

Then Mattie says, "I remember something else. I remember that we're hungry. Really **HUNGRY**."

"Look!" shouts Alex. He points at the **BOOK** that he had found in the rubbish bin.

One of the letters has changed.

Now the book's cover reads **EATS**.

AUTHOR

Michael Dahl is the author of more than 200 books for children and young adults. He has won the AEP Distinguished Achievement Award three times for his non-fiction. His Finnegan Zwake mystery series was shortlisted twice by the Anthony and Agatha awards. He has also written the Library of Doom series. He is a featured speaker at conferences on graphic novels and high-interest books for boys.

ILLUSTRATOR

Bradford Kendall has enjoyed drawing for as long as he can remember. As a boy, he loved to read comic books and watch old monster movies. He graduated from university with a BFA in Illustration. He has owned his own commercial art business since 1983, and lives with his wife, Leigh, and their two children, Lily and Stephen. They also have a cat named Hansel a dog named Gretel.

GLOSSARY

chamber large room

forms shapes

gigantic huge, enormous

guardian someone who protects a person or a place

horror fear, terror, or shock

original first

priceless very valuable

rodent mammal with large, sharp front teeth that it uses for gnawing things

rummage look for something

sewer large, underground pipe

sprout grow quickly

valuable worth a lot of money

vibrations very small, fast movements back and forth

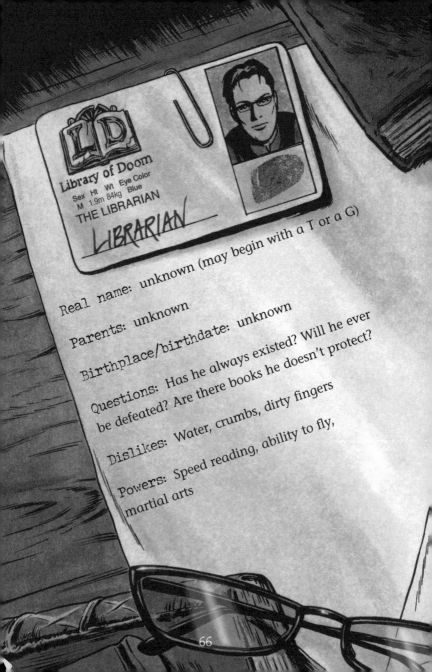

Library of Doom
Sex Ht Wt Eye Color
M 1.9m 84kg Blue
THE LIBRARIAN

LIBRARIAN

Real name: unknown (may begin with a T or a G)

Parents: unknown

Birthplace/birthdate: unknown

Questions: Has he always existed? Will he ever
be defeated? Are there books he doesn't protect?

Dislikes: Water, crumbs, dirty fingers

Powers: Speed reading, ability to fly,
martial arts

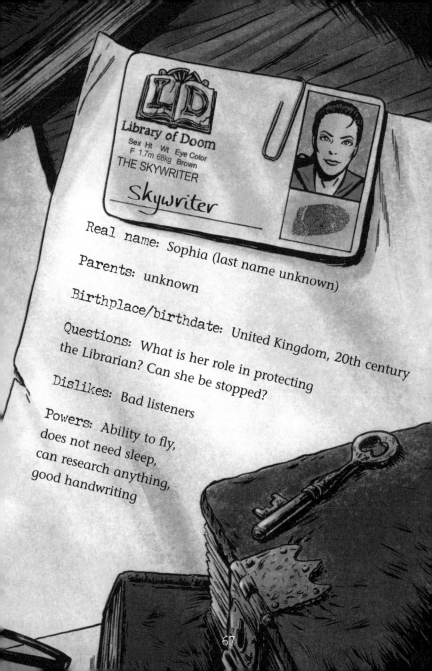

Library of Doom

Sex Ht Wt Eye Color
F 1.7m 68kg Brown
THE SKYWRITER

Skywriter

Real name: Sophia (last name unknown)

Parents: unknown

Birthplace/birthdate: United Kingdom, 20th century

Questions: What is her role in protecting the Librarian? Can she be stopped?

Dislikes: Bad listeners

Powers: Ability to fly, does not need sleep, can research anything, good handwriting

SPELLBINDER

The Spellbinder and the Librarian have battled before. In their first fight, the Spellbinder created a devious trap: once someone read a certain comic book near a scroll he had disguised to look like an ordinary grain silo, the scroll would unravel. The scroll would continue to open until it had covered the entire world.

Luckily, the Librarian discovered the evil plot before the Spellbinder's scroll could destroy the planet.

The Librarian and the Spellbinder are sworn enemies. Although the Librarian and Skywriter have defeated the Spellbinder again, he may return . . .

DISCUSSION QUESTIONS

1. Why was the Spellbinder trapping children?

2. In the first scene of this book, Alex and Mattie are looking through RUBBISH bins. What do you think they're looking for?

3. What did you think about the title of this book? Does it match what you felt when you read the story? Can you think of other titles that would be a good fit for this book?

WRITING PROMPTS

1. Imagine that the Spellbinder has turned you into a **RAT**. What is it like? What do you see, feel, hear, and smell? What do you do? How is it different from being a human?

2. In the last scene of the book, Alex and Mattie have discovered a **MAGICAL** book that gives them food. Write about a made-up book of your own that gives you something. What does it give you? Why do you like it? What is the title of your book?

3. Create a **COVER** for a book. It can be this book or another book you like, or a made-up book. Don't forget to write the information on the back, and include the author and illustrator names!

More books from the Library of Doom

Attack of the Paper Bats
The Beast Beneath the Stairs
The Book that Dripped Blood
Cave of the Bookworms
The Creeping Bookends
Escape from the Pop-up Prison
The Eye in the Graveyard
The Golden Book of Death
Poison Pages
The Smashing Scroll
The Twister Trap
The Word Eater